Chowder Rules!

The True Story of an Epic Food Fight

Enjoy this food fight!!

Anna Crowley Redding

Written by Anna Crowley Redding   Illustrated by Vita Lane

ISLANDPORT PRESS

ISLANDPORT PRESS

Islandport Press
P.O. Box 10
Yarmouth, Maine 04096
info@islandportpress.com
www.islandportpress.com

ISBN: 978-1-944762-82-7
Library of Congress Control Number: 2019946193
Printed in China.

Vermont

Ha

Massachusetts

New
York

Connecticut

Rhod
Island

Maine

For Sally, Will, Brady, Crowley, and Quinn
—Anna Crowley Redding

For James
—Vita Lane

Cleveland Sleeper, Jr. could not wait
to dive into his bowl of clam chowder.

steamy
creamy
dreamy

Clam Chowder

With just one warm, wafting whiff, Cleveland felt
like a little boy again, sitting in his mother's kitchen.
He cherished the precious tradition found in every
serving, every slurp, every sniff.

And he wasn't alone. Treasuring clam chowder was as serious as rooting for the Red Sox.

Far more than just a serving of chowder, it was the taste of comfort. In fact, it was the entire state of Maine in a single bite: sea clams, potatoes, and salt pork—all swimming in a milky broth.

Perfection.

Which is why some rotten rumor from
New York City had Cleveland seeing **RED**.
And the more he thought about it, the more
steamed he got.

Apparently the fancy and fashionable people
of the Big Apple thought it oh so ooh-la-la to
plunk (and this is hard to say) **tomatoes** into
their chowder pots.

Even worse?
They were calling
this red liquid *Manhattan*
clam chowder. Cleveland
knew exactly what he'd call it.
Vegetable soup.

Ugh!

It's

pollution!

It's

poison!

It's a

CRIME against COOKERY!

Then he began to smile. A crime. Hmm. Yes, indeed,
it should be a crime. Vile and acidic . . . just like the tomato!

As a lawmaker for the state of Maine, Cleveland was just the man to make it an official crime. He could not get himself to the State House fast enough.

After all, any man worth his weight in salt, cream, clams, and potatoes could not let this go on!

Tapping away at his typewriter,
Cleveland laid it out word for word . . .

Anyone caught poisoning the chowder cauldron with tomatoes will be forced to

dig a barrel of clams at HIGH TIDE!

The perfect punishment because it's absolutely impossible!

Cleveland called a press conference. He read the proposed bill out loud to a crowd of reporters. No taste-tainting tomato would tarnish clam chowder in the state of Maine. EVER!

The next day, when newspapers hit doorsteps from Cleveland's house clear to California, the headlines screamed:

Chowder of Maine In Peril!

1939

CLAM CHOWDER PURIST!

Before Cleveland could even file the bill, the entire country found itself in hot water.

From town to town, neighbor to neighbor, and sometimes even under the same roof, people stewed over the question:

TOMATO OR

NO TOMATO?

Cleveland's phone rang off the hook.

One of those calls was from Harry Tully, a famous Philadelphia restaurateur, a tomato lover with a big idea: Don't make a new law. Don't make tomato plunking a crime.

Instead, Harry challenged Cleveland to a *duel*.

With ladles in lieu of pistols, and armed with their very own chefs, the two men would settle the matter fair and square with a good old-fashioned cook-off—

at one of Portland, Maine's finest hotels.

In the weeks leading up to the big duel,
the nationwide food fight only grew hotter.

Cleveland whipped the matter into a frenzy.
He campaigned for Maine's culinary mascot,
giving interviews and even debating superstar
New York Yankees outfielder (and tomato sympathizer)
Joe DiMaggio *live* on the radio.

Tickets to the cook-off
sold like hot cakes.

Finally, the appointed hour arrived.

Two hundred people sat in the audience to see the contest in person. Many more sat by their radios at home, waiting to hear the live broadcast.

Cleveland and his chef entered the stage to a blinding burst of flashbulbs and a rolling newsreel camera.

Standing over their steaming cauldrons, adding a dash of this, a dash of that, and a tomato . . . or not . . . each team whisked, stirred, and salted

On the judge's panel were five famous food buffs and VIPs, including Maine Governor Lewis O. Barrows and Ruth Wakefield, the woman who invented the chocolate chip cookie.

They sniffed,

swished,

savored,

and swallowed.

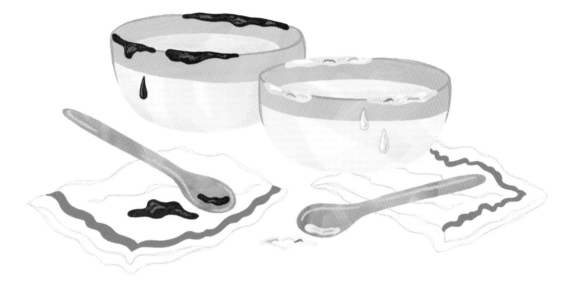

Cleveland waited.

Tomato or no tomato?
New England or Manhattan?
A hush fell over the crowd.
The judges made their decision.
And the winner?

New England Clam Chowder!

Cleveland savored the satisfaction. He'd saved the precious Maine tradition: steamy, creamy, dreamy perfection. Score squarely settled no laws required—just second helpings.

The Winning Recipe

8 good-sized potatoes
2 quarts of clam broth
1 pound of salt pork
6 medium-sized onions
6 ounces of butter
2 quarts of good Maine clams
1 quart of milk
Season with salt and pepper

Makes 6-8 servings

While the original cooking instructions are lost to history, Trent Seib, one of Maine's top chefs, recommends these steps to transform the ingredients into delicious clam chowder. He also adds a modern take on the recipe by using two tablespoons of olive oil to cook the salt pork.

Dice the potatoes. Cover in clam broth, bring to a boil, cook until soft. Dice pork to medium size. Sauté for 6 to 8 minutes in 2 tablespoons olive oil. Dice onions to medium size. In large pot, add onions and butter, and cook until onions are translucent. Add clams and milk. Bring to a boil. Fold in cooked potatoes, clam broth, and pork. Season with salt and pepper to taste.

It should be noted that the losing recipe included non-Maine clams, gallons of tomatoes, gallons of water, green peppers, celery, leeks, crushed black pepper, cayenne pepper, thyme, ketchup, parsley, salt, and sweet marjoram.

Was Cleveland Sleeper Serious?

When Cleveland Sleeper proposed this bill in 1939, he said, "Real Maine chowder is responsible for a major portion of the $100,000,000 that tourists spend in this state each year." He went on to explain his fear that if you change the chowder, tourists won't have a reason to come to Maine. But, in order to make a bill a law, it has to go through a lengthy process in both Maine's House of Representatives and Senate, which includes a first reading, second reading, engrossment, and enactment. Both the House and the Senate must vote on a bill and then send it to the Governor's desk to be signed into law. Sleeper's proposed bill never made it that far.

To Sleeper, the chowder cook-off seemed a better way to settle the problem. Who knows what would have happened if New England clam chowder didn't win!

One 1939 newspaper article on the controversy said that the state of Maine "loves publicity as a wolf loves meat." And yet the same reporter admitted that the men's "better natures were truly involved. They knew what they learned at their mothers' knees . . . that to put tomatoes into a clam chowder is to commit a crime against nature."

The state of Iowa did not find any of this remotely funny. The newspaper editor ran an editorial slamming Maine's proposed law, saying the government did not belong in the kitchen. It's worth noting that Iowa had a huge tomato industry at the time.

Even today, if you ask around, the debate continues. And opinions are usually just as passionate, urgent, and energetic as Cleveland Sleeper's.

SELECTED BIBLIOGRAPHY
"Chowder Discord." *Daily Boston Globe* 28 Feb. 1939: 14. Print.
"Maine Clam Chowder Is Winner in Contest with 'Alien' Tomato." *Portland Press Herald*
   [Portland, Maine] 4 Mar. 1939: 1-2. Print.
Beard, James. *James Beard's American Cookery*. Boston: Little, Brown, 1972. Print
Sifton, Sam. "The Clam Chowder Wars." *The New York Times Magazine*, 10 Aug. 2014: 44. Web.

About the Author: Anna Crowley Redding is an Emmy-award winning investigative television reporter, anchor, and journalist. The recipient of multiple Edward R. Murrow awards and recognized by the Associated Press for her reporting, Anna now focuses on digging up great stories for kids—which, as it turns out, is her true passion. She is the author of the young adult nonfiction titles, *Google It!* and *Elon Musk: A Mission to Save the World*, and the picture book, *Rescuing the Declaration of Independence*. For more about the cook-off, visit annacrowleyredding.com.

About the Artist: Vita Lane is a children's book illustrator. She has created artwork for a wide variety of projects including quilting fabric, wedding invitations, an animated music video, puzzles, and more. This is her first picture book.